A First-Start® Easy Reader

This easy reader contains only 57 different words,
repeated often to help the young reader develop
word recognition and interest in reading.

Basic word list for *Here Comes Winter*

a	good	says
any	have	shopping
away	he	*snip*
bag	*hip-hop*	special
big	his	store
Billy	I	the
Brrr	in	this
busy	into	three
but	is	Tilly
buttons	little	two
cloth	lots	what
coat	make	will
coming	Milly	Willy
do	new	winter
full	of	yes
get	on	you
gets	one	*zip*
go	pretty	zipper
goes	ready	zippers

Here Comes Winter

Written by Janet Craig

Illustrated by G. Brian Karas

Troll Associates

Library of Congress Cataloging in Publication Data

———

Here comes winter.

(A First-start easy reader)
Summary: When the weather turns cold, Billy the
rabbit buys the materials to make a coat.
[1. Shopping—Fiction. 2. Coats—Fiction. 3. Rabbits
—Fiction] I. Karas, G. Brian, ill. II. Title.
III. Series.
PZ7.P1762He   1988   [E]   87-13738
ISBN 0-8167-1225-5 (lib. bdg.)
ISBN 0-8167-1226-3 (pbk.)

10 9 8 7 6

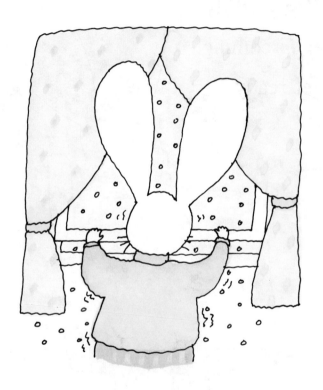

Brrr! Is winter coming?

"Brrr!" says Billy.

"Winter *is* coming.

I will get ready."

Billy gets busy.

He gets a bag—a special shopping bag.

What will Billy get?

Hip-hop. Into the store goes Billy.

"Do you have any buttons?"
says Billy.

"Yes," says Milly.

"I have lots of buttons.

Big buttons, little buttons.

Pretty buttons, special buttons."

"Good," says Billy.

"I will get three pretty buttons."

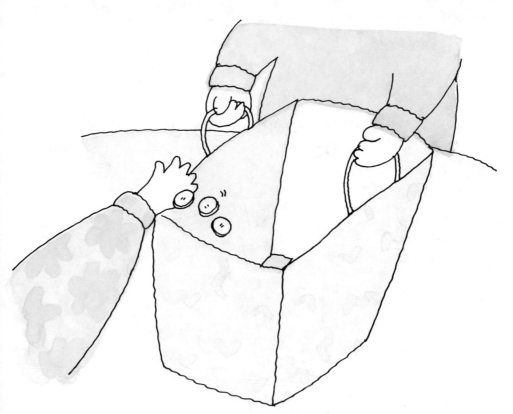

One, two, three—into the bag
go three pretty buttons.

Hip-hop. Away goes Billy.

Into the store goes Billy.

What will Billy get?

"Do you have any cloth?" says Billy.

"Yes," says Willy.

"I have lots of cloth.

Big cloth, little cloth.

Pretty cloth, special cloth."

"Good," says Billy.

"I will get special cloth."

Into the bag goes the special cloth.

Hip-hop. Away goes Billy.

Into the store goes Billy.

"Do you have any zippers?"

says Billy.

"Yes," says Tilly.

"I have lots of zippers.

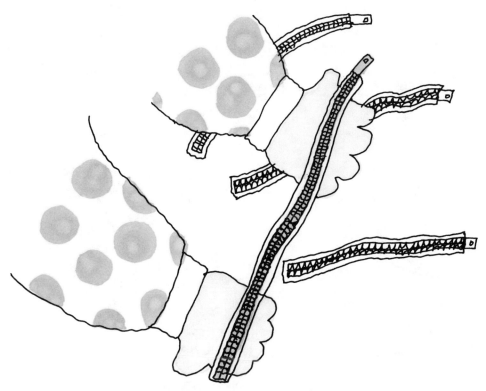

Big zippers, little zippers.

Pretty zippers, special zippers.''

"Good," says Billy.

"I will get this big zipper."

Into the bag goes the zipper.

Hip-hop. Away goes Billy.

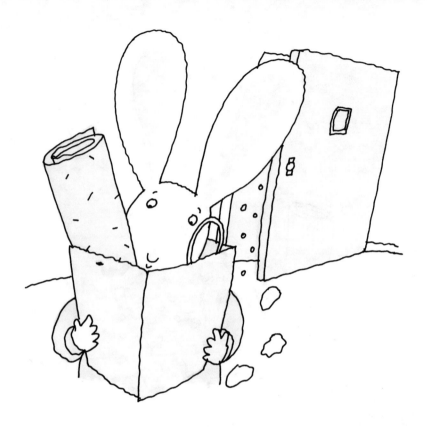

"Good," says Billy.

"The shopping bag is full."

Billy gets busy.

What will Billy make?

He gets the special cloth. *Snip, snip.*

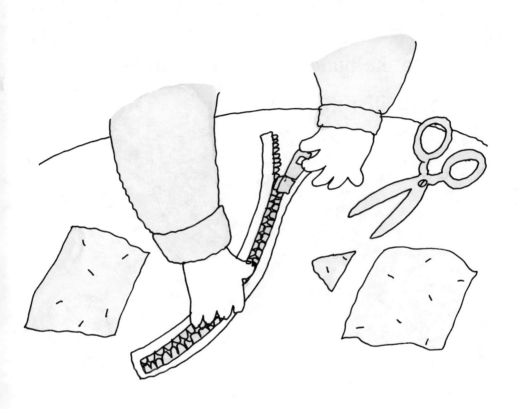

He gets the big zipper. *Zip, zip.*

On go the buttons—one, two, three.

What will Billy make?

A new coat!

Brrr! Winter is coming.

But Billy is ready in his new coat!